ANGEL CAT SUGAR

A New Friend

By Ellie O'Ryan
Illustrated by Sachiho Hino

ANGEL CAT SUGAR
characters created by Yuko Shimizu

SCHOLASTIC INC.
New York   Toronto   London   Auckland
Sydney   Mexico City   New Delhi   Hong Kong

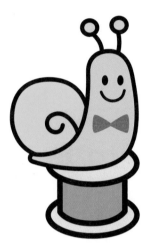

ISBN: 978-0-545-16393-4

ANGEL CAT SUGAR © 2009 YUKO SHIMIZU / TACT.C.INC.

ANGEL CAT SUGAR and all related characters and elements are trademarks of and © YUKO SHIMIZU / TACT.C.INC. All rights reserved.

Published by Scholastic Inc. SCHOLASTIC and associated logos are trademarks and/or registered trademarks of Scholastic Inc.

12 11 10 9 8 7 6 5 4 3 2   40   9 10 11 12 13 14/0

Printed in the U.S.A.
First printing, October 2009

Crash!

Lightning flashes in the sky.

The rain comes pouring down.

Angel Cat Sugar is worried.

"I hope my friends are okay!" she says.

At last, the rain stops.
The sun peeks out
from behind the clouds.

Sugar runs outside
to see her friends.
"Here they come!" she says.

Parsley wants to count
all the colors of the rainbow.
He is curious about everything!

"Count with me!" Parsley says.
"One, two, three, four,
five, six, seven!"

"Look at the birds!" Thyme says.
"They are playing in the puddles.
Let's play with them!"

Thyme makes friends wherever he goes.

Basil loves being outside—
and she loves to have fun!
"I want to jump in the puddles,
too!" Basil says. **Splash!**

Sugar wants to count the colors, meet the birds, and jump in the puddles, too. But first she wants to make sure that everyone is warm and dry after the big storm.

Helping others is what Sugar does best!

"Oh, dear!" Sugar says.
She finds a snail who needs help right away.
"This poor little snail is cold and wet!"

"The wind blew away his house. Now he has nowhere to live," she cries.

Sugar wants to help the snail.
She tucks him in her purse
and hurries home.

Sugar's friends come with her.
They want to help, too!

Sugar makes a comfy bed
out of cotton balls.
The snail will be dry
in no time!

Basil, Thyme, Sugar, and Parsley
warm up with hot chocolate.

Sugar wonders what the snail
would like to eat.
"I know where to look," says Parsley.
"In a book!"

Carrots

Apples

"Snails like to eat
carrots, apples, and grapes,"
Parsley says.
The snail thinks that sounds yummy!

Snails

Grapes

"Carrots, apples, and grapes
grow in my garden!" Basil says.

Basil hurries to her garden
to get some food for the snail.

Thyme can tell that the snail is sad.
"I'll cheer you up!" he says.
"Watch me juggle!"
Parsley and Sugar giggle.

Sugar knows that the snail needs
a new place to live.
He needs a warm, dry house of his own.
How can she help the snail?

Then Sugar has a great idea.
She can make him a new house!
She gets a big box.
She turns it into a tiny house
for the tiny snail!

"You need a name, too,"
Sugar says to the snail.
"We can call you Cinnamon!"
The snail likes his new name!

Now Cinnamon has everything he needs—
yummy food,
a new house,
a new name . . .

And some very special new friends!